MW00939975

MY
MOM IS A
SPY!

For GG and BapBap (for the inspiration),
Squirrel (for setting the scene) and
little F and O (for all the best plot twists).
Jess French

Published in 2022 by Welbeck Flame
An imprint of Welbeck Children's Limited,
Part of Welbeck Publishing Group.
Based in London and Sydney.

ISBN: 978 1 80130 0308

Printed and bound by CPI Group (UK)
10 9 8 7 6 5 4 3 2 1

ANDY MCNAB
JESS FRENCH

ILLUSTRATED BY NATHAN REED

Idris sighed. When Mom had told him that Lucía was coming to stay for spring break, he had prepared himself to share the TV remote and maybe some of his model animals, but he had not prepared himself for this.

"Are you ready?" Lucía asked, bouncing excitedly. There was a scrap of paper clenched in her hand, which she was waving wildly from side to side.

"No," Idris said, turning his back on Lucía and storming out of the room. He didn't make it far before a loud crunch stopped him in his tracks.

"Ouch!" he yelled, looking down to see a small plastic object crushed beneath his tiger slippers. From behind him, Lucía let out a loud squeal.

"My spy drone!" she cried. "Please tell me that wasn't my spy drone."

"Er..." said Idris, thrusting his hands into his pockets. "It was an accident."

"Nooo," she wailed, dropping to her knees and gathering the broken pieces.

Philby, Lucía's scruffy brown dog, bounded into the room and started sniffing around the scene of the crime.

"Get away, Philby," Lucía said.

"Come here, Philbs," said Idris softly, calling the dog toward him. Philby was the only good thing about Lucía coming to stay. For as long as Idris could remember, he had begged Mom for a dog, but she

TIGERS

had always said no. Mom was more of a cat person. Unfortunately for Mom, when she had fallen in love with Lucía's dad, she'd had to accept that whenever they came to stay, Philby would come too.

"It's OK," Lucía said, "you just broke one of the propellers. With a bit of superglue it will soon be as good as new."

"Oh phew," said Idris sarcastically. "So glad that you will still be interrupting *Creature Feature* with the buzzing of that useless machine for the rest of the week."

Creature Feature was Idris's favorite television program. Hosted by Jungle Jack, it was packed full of incredible animal facts. Jungle Jack was Idris's idol, and one day, Idris hoped to be a wildlife presenter just like him. Or maybe a vet. He wasn't entirely sure yet; all he knew was that he would definitely work with animals, preferably outside. He couldn't imagine anything worse than being stuck in an office all day, like his mom.

"So now will you listen to me?" Lucía asked.

"I already told you," Idris said. "I'm not interested."

"Well, I'm going to read it to you anyway," Lucía said. She cleared her throat and began, "Reasons that Sarah is a spy. Number one..."

"**Arrrgh**," growled Idris.

Could Lucía be any more annoying? When she'd been obsessed with sports cars back in the summer, she'd been unbearable. She'd zoomed around the apartment, screeching around corners and reversing quickly down the hallway. But this was worse. Lucía's latest obsession was spies.

She wouldn't talk about anything else. She spent her days creeping around, listening through doors, writing codes, and scribbling down anything that she considered to be a clue. Worst of all, she was convinced that Idris's *mom* was a spy.

Idris stomped into his bedroom and slammed the door. He could hear Lucía banging on the other side and knew that he was risking another complaint from Mrs. Jones next door, but he didn't care. He'd had enough. He scanned the room for his headphones, catching snatches of what Lucía was shouting as they drifted through the door...

"...crossword champion ... different name ... car chase ... five languages..."

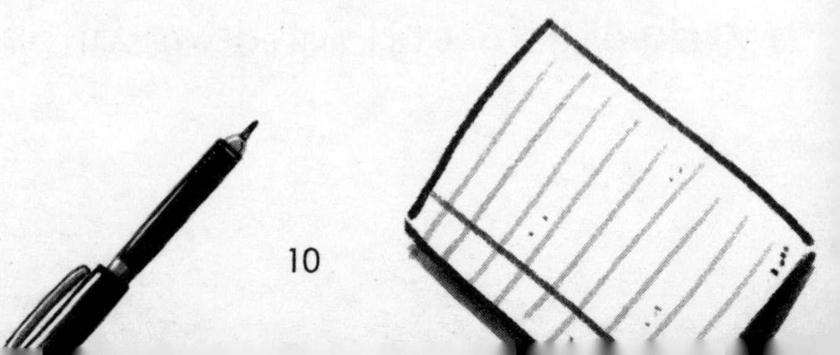

He hurried over to his desk, which stood below a poster of an orangutan. Ah, there were his headphones. He thrust them over his ears and the sound of Lucía's voice was drowned out immediately. Idris looked at the orangutan poster and sighed.

"I bet you've never had this problem, have you?" he asked. "You're a solitary male. You spend almost all of your time alone in the treetops."

Idris wished he could live alone in the trees. He barely ever got to spend time in the wild. There was a nature reserve just out of town, but his mom was usually too busy working to take him.

"That's Lucía," he said to the orangutan, jerking his head toward the bedroom door. "Annoying, isn't she?"

He sighed and sat down at his desk.

"Oh, and to top it all off..." He put his head in his hands. "She thinks my mom is a spy."

He almost laughed at how ridiculous it was. His mom was the furthest thing from a spy he could imagine. He could list a million reasons why she would make a terrible spy. In fact, that was exactly what he would do! He sat up straight and started to ferret through the messy piles on top of his desk until he found his notebook. He flicked past his notes on rattlesnake venom and found the first clean page, then wrote:

REASONS MY MOM IS ABSOLUTELY, DEFINITELY 100% NOT A SPY

1. She works fifty hours a week at Bingo Blotts' Paperclip Factory – when would she have time to be a spy?
2. The last time she exercised was a Zumba class at the village hall when I was five.
3. She can barely deliver a lamb chop, let alone a karate chop.
4. She is useless with technology. She doesn't even own a smartphone.
5. Her idea of an exciting day out is going to the zoo and spending three hours watching the guinea pigs.

Idris sat back and cracked his knuckles. He felt a bit better after writing his list. He almost felt guilty about slamming the door on Lucía.

The problem was, when Lucía insisted that his mom was a spy, it just reminded Idris of how *boring* and *ordinary* his mom was. Lucía would never understand how that felt. Lucía's dad was an *exotic animal vet!* **COOLEST. JOB. IN. THE. WORLD.**

It was the smell of sizzling onions that finally drew Idris out of his room. He stepped out of his doorway onto something soft and warm.

"**Aroof!**" yelped Philby, who had been lying outside his door, chewing a squeaky toy crab.

"Oh, Philby," said Idris, dropping to his knees. "I'm sorry, I didn't see you there." Philby licked his face in acceptance and together they trotted down the hallway. In the kitchen, Lucía and her dad were busy making dinner. Idris glanced around at the piles of dirty bowls and Philby hurried to lick a stream of tomato sauce that was dribbling down the front of the cupboards. Mom wouldn't be happy about all this mess. Oh well, it made a nice change to eat home-cooked food.

"Hi, David," Idris said.

Lucía's dad turned, smiling. "Hey, Idris," he said. "We're making enchiladas."

"Smells good," Idris replied.

"Don't worry," said Lucía, holding out a smaller bowl. "I'm making you some without cheese." Idris gave her what he hoped was a grateful smile. One of the only benefits of the Garcías coming to stay was the food. With Mom it was usually frozen pizzas or baked potatoes and occasionally fish and chips, but when David and Lucía came to stay, every meal was a celebration.

"Yum!" Idris grinned. "How was the zoo today, David? What animals did you see?"

"Oh, you know," David replied. "Busy. Do you remember I told you about the lion cubs that were born a few weeks ago?"

"Yes!" said Idris, nodding enthusiastically. David had shown him some screenshots from the camera they had placed inside the enclosure. They had captured footage of the lioness giving birth. It had been even better than watching *Creature Feature!*

"Well, one of the cubs has been rejected by its mother. We've had to take it away so that it can be hand reared by one of the zookeepers. He's named it Moshi."

"That's so sad," said Idris. "Why would its mother reject it?"

"It can happen for all sorts of reasons,"

said David. "But in this case I think Zahara, Moshi's mother, could sense that he was unwell. When I examined Moshi I found that he had a viral infection. He will need some intense treatment to get it under control."

"Will he get better?" Lucía asked.

"He should," said David, "but by then it will be too late for him to go back to Zahara."

"So what will happen to Moshi once he's stronger?" asked Idris.

"He will probably end up in another zoo somewhere," said David. "I'm not sure yet, I've been busy dealing with Budi the orangutan. He's been under the weather for several days now."

"Oh no," said Idris, "what's wrong with him?"

"I don't know," said David. "I'm going to take some more samples from him tomorrow. Everything I've tested so far has been totally normal." He paused as Lucía held out a spoonful of tomato sauce for him to taste. He slurped loudly, then clapped his hands together triumphantly. "Perfect!"

Lucía beamed, then turned to Idris.

"Could you set the table please?"

Idris swept a pile of assorted papers and toys from the table into a heap on the floor and set out the placemats and cutlery with pride.

David placed a steaming plate in the center of the table.

"Have you heard from your mom, Idris?" he asked.

Idris shook his head.

"No, but she won't be home yet, she's never home before—" He was cut short by the sound of the front door opening.

"Sarah!" David smiled. "Just in time for dinner."

"Hi, everyone," Mom said, dumping her bag and keys onto a side table. "Wow, doesn't this all look delicious." She kissed Idris on the head before squeezing into the chair beside him and switched on the small television that sat behind the table.

"I want to hear all about your days," Mom said, "but can we just quickly watch the news before we eat?"

She didn't wait for an answer. The screen crackled to life and the image of a scaly brown animal flashed onto the screen, with the words *Theft at Central Zoo* below it.

Idris and Lucía gasped.

"Is that your zoo, Papi?" Lucía asked.

David nodded silently, his eyes wide behind his glasses and his thick eyebrows

raised high. Out of the corner of his eye, Idris saw Mom's hand go to her chest.

"You OK, Mom?" he asked.

She nodded. "Fine, sweetheart."

"This is the breaking story of the theft of three Sunda pangolins from Central Zoo, thought to be the work of an international smuggling ring."

"What's a pangolin?" asked Lucía.

"The world's only scaly mammal," said Idris quickly, his eyes not moving from the television screen. "There are eight different species across Africa and Asia."

"They're pretty cute," said Lucía. A pangolin walked across the screen, tottering on its hind legs, hands tucked up in front of its chest.

"Extremely." Idris nodded. "And critically endangered." The walking pangolin was replaced by a picture of a suitcase. Inside were dozens of curled-up pangolins.

"Why would someone steal a pangolin?" asked Lucía.

"They are sold for their scales and meat," said Idris. "They are the most illegally trafficked mammals in the world."

"Did you know the pangolins had been stolen, Papi?" Lucía asked.

David shook his head. "This is the first I'm hearing of it. I'd better check my phone..."

David got up, walked across to his coat, and rummaged through the pockets. Suddenly a shrill bell rang out in the hallway. The doorbell.

"I'll get that," said Mom, leaping to her feet.

Lucía darted a knowing look at Idris. "*Spy stuff,*" she mouthed.

Idris rolled his eyes.

Moments later, Mom returned.

"Wrong apartment," she said. Idris noted a flamingo-pink piece of paper sticking out of her pocket. Had that been there before? He hadn't noticed.

"I have an idea," said Mom, lifting a forkful of enchilada to her mouth. "I think we all need cheering up. We haven't been to the zoo for a long time, have we, Idris?"

Idris shook his head.

"We should go!" she said. "Would you like that, kids? How about tomorrow? We could come and visit you, David."

"Tomorrow?" said David, frowning again. "Tomorrow is not so good—

I have all the samples to take from the orangutan and..."

"I'm sure Idris would love to help you," said Mom. "Wouldn't you, Idris?"

Idris's palms started to sweat. He passed the zoo almost every day on the bus; it was two stops before his school. But he couldn't remember the last time he had been inside. The truth was, he wasn't sure what he thought of zoos. All those captive animals...In his opinion, no animal belonged in a cage.

David seemed to read his thoughts.

"You know, I don't love the thought of captive animals either," he said. "But right now, while their wild habitat is in such a poor state, good zoos are the best option for some species. Why don't you come and see their big new enclosures before you make up your mind?'

Idris remembered the documentaries he had seen about palm oil. Until humans started to treat the forests better, there wasn't much left for orangutans in the wild. Maybe he could go to the zoo once, just to see what it was like . . .

"Come on, Idris," said Lucía. "It will be great fun. And while we're there we can look into the disappearance of the pangolins."

"All right," said Idris. "Just this once. But if the animals look unhappy I'm coming straight home." Lucía punched the air and gave a little whoop of excitement.

"That sounds fair," said David. "You never know, visitors might even do Budi some good."

"Do you think we will get to see Moshi the lion cub, too?" Lucía asked hopefully.

David shook his head.

"Moshi is being kept off-site at the moment," he said. "In the home of one of the zookeepers. Oh, and don't forget the zoo is only open until lunchtime on Wednesdays."

"No problem," said Mom, through a mouthful of enchilada. "I'll bring the kids over at ten."

Chapter Three

"Come on, Idris," shouted Mom. "We're going to be late!"

He piled one last textbook into his already full backpack and headed into the kitchen.

"Goodness, Idris. Do you really need to bring all those books?"

"It's not just books," he replied, "it's my camera too." Just then, Lucía bounded into the room, knocking his backpack to the ground.

"Sorry," she squealed, bending down to help him pick it up. "I'm just *too* excited that I am going to start solving my very first spy mission today."

"Do you really think anyone is going to tell you anything about the pangolins?" said Idris. "You're just a kid. They have special detectives for that kind of thing."

"Aha," replied Lucía. "I may look like 'just a kid,' but I have two things on my side that those detectives don't."

She opened the orange utility belt that was strapped around her waist. "Firstly, spy gear."

Idris peered inside the pocket. There were a few pens, a magnifying glass, some paperclips, a flashlight, some small round batteries, and a scruffy notebook.

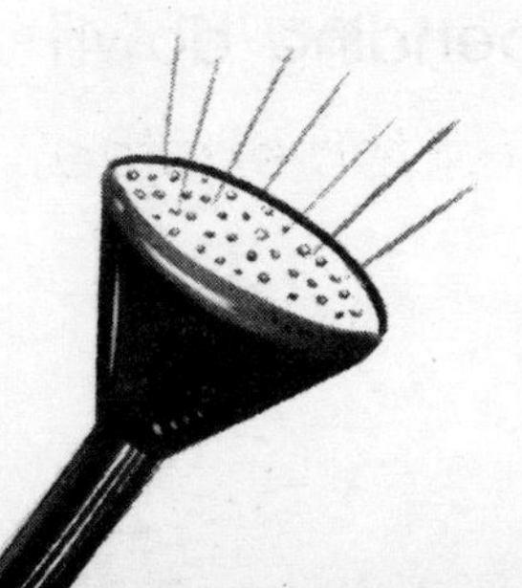

"What are the batteries for?" Idris asked.

"In case I need to replace the batteries in my hearing aid," said Lucía. "There's no way I would let that stop my mission!"

"Great attitude," said Mom. "What's the second thing?"

"The element of surprise," replied Lucía. "No one would ever expect a sweet little girl to be capable of solving crimes, so I can get away with things that other people can't."

Idris stifled a laugh. He wasn't sure he would have described Lucía as a 'sweet little girl.' She was more like a hawk, hovering around the apartment, diving speedily onto anything she thought might be a clue. Luckily, Mom interrupted before Idris could tell her that.

"Now, before we go," Mom said, helping Idris to heave the backpack onto his shoulders, "remind me what you must do if you urgently need to contact me or David and we aren't answering our phones."

Idris rolled his eyes. They went through this almost every time they left the house.

"Firstly, make sure we are both safe, then open the emergency tin."

"Mm-hmm," said Mom, nodding approvingly. "And where is that, Lucía?"

Lucía pointed to a rusty metal candy can that sat on top of the kitchen cupboards.

"What's inside it?" Lucía whispered to Idris.

"Let's hope you never have to find

out," replied Mom. "Come on, let's go."

They traipsed out of the apartment and down to the parking lot, which was in the basement. Idris made sure to slide into the seat behind Mom—some of his animal books were stored in the pocket on the back of her seat.

A few minutes later, they were strapped into the car and on their way. As they were pulling out onto the highway, the air was suddenly filled with an angry

roaring sound. Idris looked around in alarm. The noise grew louder and louder until the whole car began shaking.

"McLaren 570GT," Lucía whispered, her voice quivering with excitement. "I would know that sound anywhere."

Idris followed her gaze out of the window. What on earth was a McLaren 570GT? A blur of purple zoomed past, causing the oncoming traffic to swerve and honk their horns.

"Look at her go," Lucía sighed. A car! Of course.

The purple sports car zoomed off into the distance. Idris shook his head, then buried it back into his book. He had barely read a paragraph when Lucía interrupted him again.

"Still don't believe me?" Lucía hissed, pointing at Sarah. Idris looked over at Mom; she had her eyes fixed on the road and didn't seem to be doing anything unusual.

"Believe you about what?" he whispered back.

"She's driven around this roundabout three times already," Lucía said. "I know exactly what she's doing. It's called an *anti-surveillance drill*. It's something you do to make sure nobody is following you." Idris rolled his eyes. He wished

Lucía would drop the spy stuff.

"She's probably just forgotten which exit to take," Idris said. "Look, she's indicating now."

"There's something strange going on," muttered Lucía. "I just know it."

Moments later, Mom pulled over outside a news stand.

"Everything OK, Sarah?" Lucía asked.

"Yes, dear," said Mom, "I just suddenly had the fear that I had forgotten my purse. But look—" She held aloft a brown leather pouch. "It's right here. Silly me, I would forget my head if it wasn't screwed on."

Idris knew that Lucía was trying to catch his eye, so he purposefully avoided looking at her. Eventually she jabbed him in the ribs.

"What?" he squeaked.

"She's stopped to see if anyone was following us," said Lucía. "Spies do it all the time. They pull over and pretend they are doing something ordinary, like checking their phone or looking at a map, but really they are checking out their surroundings, noting down anything unusual they spot."

Idris shook his head.

"She stopped because she's forgetful." he said. "I haven't seen her write any notes, have you? And she's not looking around at all."

"She's using that mirror to look behind her," said Lucía, pointing at Sarah. "Look."

Idris glanced at Mom, who was touching up her lipstick using a compact mirror.

"She's just doing her makeup," said Idris.

"Are you telling me that makes her a spy now too?"

"Yes" said Lucía. "Yes I am." She pulled out her notebook and started scribbling again.

Idris watched out of the window as Mom pulled out into the road.

How could his mom possibly be a spy without him knowing? She would have told him if she was, he was sure of it. She hadn't been acting strangely, she had just been worried about her purse. That was totally normal behavior, wasn't it? He tried not to let his thoughts get carried away with themselves and to instead focus on all the incredible animals he was about to meet at the zoo. He had looked through the website and made a list of his top ten animals to see. At the very top of the list was the cobalt blue tarantula. He couldn't wait.

Getting to the zoo entrance took forever. Lucía noticed that the purple sports car that had passed them was parked in the parking lot and had to stop and marvel at it for several minutes. Then Mom forgot her phone and had to run back to the car. Eventually they made it to the gate. Outside, Mom passed Idris a map.

"Take a look and see where you want to go first," Mom said. "We have fifteen minutes before we are supposed to meet David."

They approached the zoo desk.

ZOO

"Where were the pangolins?" asked Lucía, grabbing the map and peering at it intently.

"That will be the Southeast Asia house, miss," said the teenage boy behind the counter. "But the pangolin exhibit is closed. I don't know if you've seen the news but—"

"Of course we have!" Lucía interrupted. "That's why we're here."

"That's not why we are here, Lucía," said Mom, glaring at Lucía. "We are here to see David García, the zoo vet. We are supposed to be meeting him in the orangutan house at ten o'clock."

"In that case, you're in luck." The boy winked at Lucía. "The pangolin exhibit and the orangutans are in the same building." He pulled out another map and drew a circle on it. "Head for the otters but take a left before you reach the gibbons. If you find yourself at the penguins then you've gone too far."

Idris took the new map, folding it carefully so that their route was on top, and led the way. The path took them through a wildflower meadow, where clouds of

butterflies fluttered around small purple flowers. Everywhere he looked, there was information about native wildlife and how to protect it.

"The zoo isn't how I remember it," said Idris, following the lazy path of a late-flying brimstone.

"Yeah, my dad says they got loads of funding," Lucía said. "They improved the enclosures and spent lots of money on trying to encourage native species."

Together, Idris, Lucía, and Mom followed the path through the wildflower meadow and took a left turn when they saw a sign for the gibbons. As they rounded the corner, the Southeast Asia house came into view. It was a beautiful building, which looked like it had also received some of that funding Lucía had mentioned.

As they approached, an impressive set of wide glass doors slid open. Idris turned to watch as they closed again behind him and was pleased to spot a sticker proclaiming:

"This place is pretty cool," he said.

Lucía grinned. "I love it!"

Both sides of the building were bordered by large glass windows. Signs indicated that the orangutans were housed on the other side of the glass, but the dense green plants in their cages made the apes difficult to spot.

The inside of the building was made to look like a palm oil plantation, with smaller glass cages dotted between resin trees and lots of signs warning about the dangers of deforestation.

"See," said Mom. "Not bad here, is it? Now, I'm just going to take a bathroom break. I will meet you by that tuk-tuk just before ten." She pointed at a brightly colored vehicle, nestled underneath a sign saying:

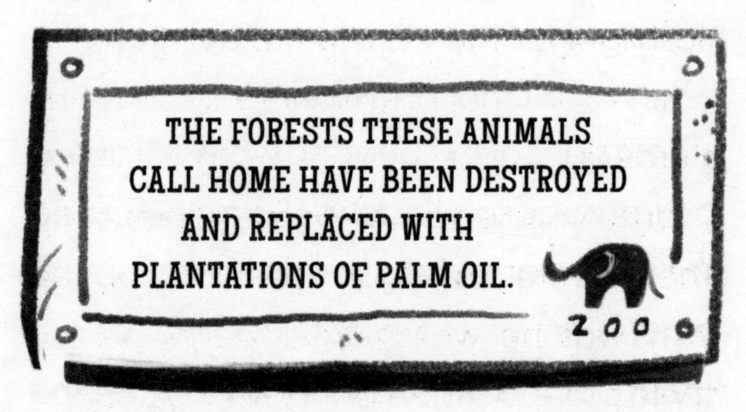

Idris nodded, looking around to see where Lucía had gone. He spotted her on all fours, peering at the edge of the sliding door with a magnifying glass.

"What are you doing?" he said, looking around nervously. "People are watching."

"Checking the entry and exit points," Lucía said. "To steal the pangolins, someone had to be able to move in and out of the building easily."

She was upside down now, shining a flashlight on the closing mechanism.

"It's on a timer and the lock looks pretty sturdy."

Idris tapped his foot impatiently. There were so many animals to see. Why was he watching a wannabe spy try to solve a stolen pangolin mystery?

"This is ridiculous," said Idris. "I'm heading over to the tarantulas. Meet me at the tuk-tuk in ten minutes."

He made his way through the fake

palm oil plantation and found a crowd of people gathered around two police officers. Idris guessed this must have been the pangolin exhibit. He skirted around the edge of the group; crowds made him feel nervous. At the back, he spotted a woman in a blue apron.

"Excuse me," said Idris, tapping her on the shoulder. "Where are the tarantulas please?"

The woman looked around sharply and brushed a strand of purple hair into her hairnet before answering. "I don't know. I'm just a cleaner."

"Ah right, sorry,"

said Idris, squinting through the crowd. At the other side he spotted Mom. That was strange; weren't the toilets near the entrance? He raised his hand to wave but she didn't look in his direction. What was she doing over there? As he watched, she moved toward a bulletin board. When she was close enough, she pushed something into the top right corner. At the risk of sounding like Lucía, that was odd behavior.

"This is it, then," said a voice from over his shoulder. Idris jumped about a foot in the air.

"You scared me!" he said. "This is what?"

"The scene of the crime," said Lucía excitedly. "Seen anything suspicious?"

Idris didn't want to add fuel to her spy story, so he didn't tell her what he had seen.

"Only you," said Idris, "creeping around

like a forensic scientist."

"Maybe one day." Lucía smiled. "I did manage to find out how the locks work, though. After visiting hours are over, they automatically seal and the only person that can open them is the on-duty zookeeper. So we just need to find out who that was on the day the pangolins were taken."

"Fascinating," said Idris in a dull, unimpressed voice.

"Oh, cheer up, Idris. What's wrong?"

"I wanted to see the cobalt blue tarantulas," he said sadly. "But there are too many people to get through."

"Cobalt blue tarantulas," Lucía said. "I saw a sign for them over here!"

She grabbed his hand and pulled him through the crowd. He held his breath and tried not to panic, grateful that Lucía was leading the way. As they approached the other side, Idris spotted the bulletin board where he had seen Mom. There was a red drawing pin stuck in the top right corner. Mom must have left it there. He looked around to see if Mom was still there and noticed another person looking at the drawing pin. It was a man in a brown hat. He had a droopy mustache, which flopped across his upper lip like a sleepy weasel. The man looked quickly at the drawing pin, ignoring the rest of the displays, then went on his way.

"What are you looking at?" asked Lucía.

"Nothing," Idris said. "Where are the tarantulas?"

Lucía flashed him a mischievous smile.

"Through here." She pointed at a small gap between the trees and the wall.

"How do you know that?" said Idris, following nervously behind her.

"I saw them when I was looking for clues," said Lucía, grunting a little as she squeezed herself through the even narrower gap at the far end. "Ah, here we are."

When they emerged on the other side of the display, Idris immediately came face to face with a large, blue tarantula.

The sight of it took his breath away.

"Those colors," he said. "Aren't they extraordinary." He pulled his camera from his bag and started snapping images. As often happened when he was photographing wildlife, Idris lost track of time. With one eye on the viewfinder and the other squeezed shut, he didn't notice when Lucía slipped away. He continued snapping and clicking and repositioning. The rest of the world melted away until it was just him, his camera, and the spider. He was so absorbed in his task that he didn't hear when footsteps approached from down the corridor. So absorbed, in fact, that he didn't even bat an eyelid when a tall man emerged from the shadows behind him and tapped him on the shoulder.

The touch of the man's hand made Idris jump out of his skin.

"What are you doing here?" the man said, in a low, gravelly voice. "This area's out of bounds."

Idris swallowed, trying to catch his breath. As his eyes adjusted to the shadowy room, the man's face came into focus. The way the light fell on his nose gave the impression of a large, hooked beak.

"Sorry," squealed Idris, leaping backward. "I didn't realize." He stuffed his camera back into his bag. "I'll go."

He looked around for Lucía. She had been there just a moment ago, hadn't she?

"I'll escort you out," said the man, narrowing his eyes. Idris noticed two long, red scratches on his right cheek. They looked very fresh.

"Yes, of course," said Idris. "I'm really sorry, I just—"

"I'm not interested in your excuses,"

said the man, stomping ahead of him, shoulders stooped like a vulture. "Just don't do it again." Idris noted a piece of paper clasped in the man's right hand. Was he going to give Idris some kind of written warning?

"There you are!" shouted Lucía as Idris and the vulture man emerged back into the open.

"Where did you get to?" Idris mumbled.

"I wanted to get another look at the pangolin enclosure," she said. "Sorry." She lowered her voice and covered her mouth so that the man could not read her lips. "Who is *that* guy? And what happened to his face?"

"I have no idea," said Idris, glancing nervously back at him. Lucía pulled the notebook from her belt pocket.

"No idea?" she grumbled. "That's no good. What am I supposed to write on my suspect list?" Before he could stop her, Lucía was tapping the man on the shoulder. "Excuse me," she asked. "Who are you?"

The man's beady eyes peered down at her over his long nose-beak and he scowled.

"Victor," he growled. "Head of wildcats. Who are you?"

"My name is Lucía," Lucía said. "And I'm investigating the mystery of the missing pangolins." Victor's scowl deepened.

"Plenty of police sniffing around doing that," he said. "We don't need kids like you poking their noses in too."

"Very sorry to have troubled you," said Idris, pulling Lucía away before she could respond. "I'll make sure to stay to the proper walkways from now on."

"Make sure you do that," said Victor as the two children hurried away. "I'll be watching."

"What a horrible man," Lucía said angrily, shaking away Idris's arm. "Victor's going straight to the top of my suspect list."

Idris and Lucía hurried over to the tuk-tuk, where Mom would surely be waiting. On the other side of the bridge, Idris caught sight of the man in the brown hat again. He lifted his cap and wiped his brow.

"There's your mom," said Lucía, pointing a few yards to the right of the man. "Come on."

As they crossed the bridge, the man

in the brown hat started moving too. Then Idris's eyes played a trick on him. For the briefest of moments, as the man in the brown hat moved past Mom, Idris thought that he had seen the man *drop something* into Mom's coat pocket! Idris shook himself. He was letting his imagination run wild.

"Are you OK?" Lucía asked, tugging on his sleeve. "You've got that weird look again."

Idris nodded.

"Just a little hungry," he said, trying to ignore the uneasy feeling in his stomach.

"Ah, there you are, children!" said Mom, hurrying toward them. "Come on, we're late; David will be waiting for us."

She led them through the building,

SOUTH EAST
ZOO

passing through the fake palm-oil plantation until they reached a door that said:

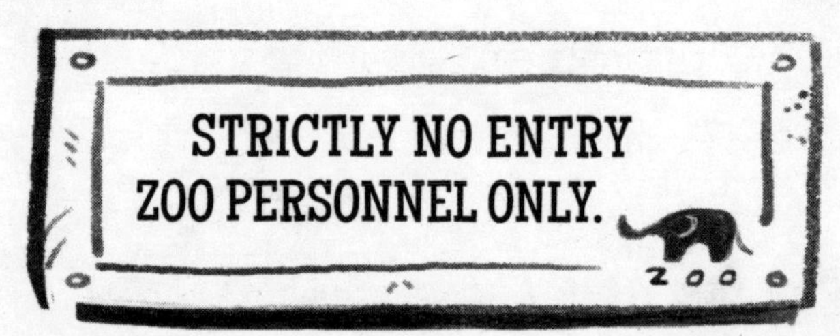

She knocked on the door. Moments later, David appeared, looking flustered. His glasses were pushed up on his head and his eyes were tinged red.

"Is it ten o'clock already?" he asked.

"Yes," said Mom.

"Everything OK, Papi?" Lucía asked.

"*Sí, sí,* just a lot to do. Welcome, welcome!" He opened the door wide for them to come past.

"I was actually going to go and look at the guinea pigs if that's all right," said Mom, moving back toward the door. "You'll be OK with the kids for a bit?"

"OK, no problem," said David, patting down his top in search of his glasses before realizing they were on top of his head. "Everything is under control."

"Great," said Mom. "Be good, I'll be back in a jiffy."

David led them through a small boot room, where he got them to dip their shoes in a blue disinfectant before leading them through a door that said *Zookeepers' area*.

The zookeepers' area was much smaller than Idris had imagined. The orangutan enclosure was so huge that Idris had expected the zookeepers to have an equally impressive space behind it.

In reality, the zookeepers' area was barely wider than the hallway of Idris's apartment. Unlike the enclosure, which was lush, green, and beautiful, this corridor was dull and gray.

"Come in," said a woman in a green uniform. She was sitting on an upturned bucket, a bunch of grapes in her lap. "Lucía, Idris," she said. "David talks so fondly about you, it's great to finally put faces to the names."

"Hi," said Lucía.

"Nice to meet you," said Idris. "Thanks for agreeing to let us come."

"This is Maira," said David. "She's the zoo manager and has been closely observing Budi over the last couple of days."

"It's been such a worry," Maira said, wringing her hands. "Our Budi is usually such a cheerful ape. But no matter what we do, we just can't seem to snap him out of it." She stood up, a single grape held between finger and thumb, and walked toward the bars. For the first time, Idris noticed the orangutan.

He was enormous. A huge, hairy, orange figure, sitting silently on the other side of a wall of wire. It was clear to see why the zookeepers were worried about him. His shoulders were drooped and he stared blankly into his lap, barely responding when Maira called his name.

"Have you found anything wrong with him?" Idris asked.

David shook his head. "Everything has come back normal. I've taken some more samples today." He held up a tray full of plastic vials. "And we will see what we find, but for now it's a mystery."

"I've tried everything," Maira said. "I've brushed his hair, given him a shower, blown bubbles, given him scrunched-up newspaper, offered him his favorite fruit..." She pointed at the pineapples and melons strewn about Budi's enclosure.

"All the things he usually likes but he's just..." She glanced sadly at Budi. "Well, look."

Idris moved up toward the bars. "He looks so sad, poor thing."

"Would you like to try feeding him?" Maira asked, holding the grape out to Idris. Idris nodded and took the fruit.

"Hey, Budi," said Idris, talking in a soft, calm voice and avoiding eye contact, as he would if he were approaching a nervous dog. Budi looked around slowly at the sound of the new voice, but did not move from his spot. "You must be hungry; come on, these grapes are delicious." But the ape did not look around again.

"What is he like when the visitors aren't here?" Idris asked, remembering how overwhelming he had found the hustle and bustle of all the people. "Could it be all the fuss around the pangolin cage?"

"Good question, Idris," said Maira. "I haven't been here after closing for the last few days."

"What about putting a camera in his cage?" Idris said. "That's what Jungle Jack does whenever he wants to see how an animal acts when he's not around."

"That's not a bad idea," said David. "We have that camera from the lion enclosure—we don't need that now that the cubs have been born."

"Great plan," said Maira. "I can check in on it from home and see what Budi is up to. Thanks, Idris. Come on, let's go and meet Indah—she's in a much better mood and she adores visitors!"

Idris's chest swelled with pride as they moved down to the next enclosure, where a young female orangutan was waiting expectantly.

"Hello, Indah," said Maira, handing the orangutan a quarter of orange. The ape took it gently in her hand, then pulled back her rubbery lips and popped it into her mouth.

"She's beautiful," said Idris. Indah turned to him, a halo of marmalade fur sticking out untidily around her face, then held out her hand.

"She wants that grape," said Maira with a laugh. "It's OK, you can give it to her."

Idris looked down at his palm nervously.

"There's no need to be afraid," said Maira. "She's very friendly."

Idris's heart was racing as he held out

the fruit for Indah to take. Maira was right, there was nothing to fear—Indah took the fruit ever so gently, then moved away from the bars, making happy little grunting noises as she went.

Beside Idris, Lucía pulled out her notebook.

"Maira," Lucía said, in a serious voice. "Do you mind if I ask you a few questions about the disappearance of the pangolins?"

"Sorry, Maira," said Idris, shaking his head. "She thinks she's going to solve the mystery all by herself."

"No need to be sorry," replied Maira. "That's excellent news. The sooner we get those darling creatures back where

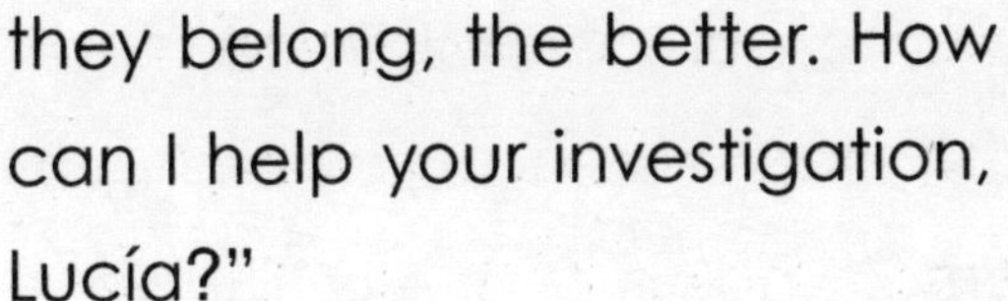

they belong, the better. How can I help your investigation, Lucía?"

Lucía smiled and consulted her notebook. "First things first, who was the on-duty zookeeper on the day the pangolins disappeared?"

Maira pointed at a bulletin board on the wall behind them.

"You will find the roster pinned up over there," she said.

Lucía walked up to the bulletin board and stared at it for a few moments.

"Gethin," she said, before scribbling the name down in her notebook.

"That's right," said Maira. "But there's no way Gethin had anything to do with the disappearance of the pangolins. Nor any of the zookeepers at Central Zoo, in fact. We love our animals more than anything else and would do anything to protect them."

"But the on-duty zookeeper is the only one who can open the doors to this building after hours," said Lucía. "No one could have gotten in without his help."

"That may be true," said Maira. "But I'm telling you it wasn't Gethin that took those pangolins. I'd bet my house on it. If someone came in from outside to steal our pangolins, Gethin didn't let them in the doors."

Lucía was still standing by the rota when Mom came rushing down the corridor.

"OK, children," she said. "Taken all your samples? It's time to go."

"But we just got here," Lucía protested. "I still have lots of leads to investigate."

"I'm afraid you'll have to come back another time," Mom said. "I have to get home to collect a package."

"You do?" Idris asked. She hadn't mentioned anything about a package this morning.

"Yes," said Mom. "I just got a text. We need to leave now."

"Is it that important?" asked Idris. "Can't we get it later?"

"Sorry, love," said Mom, placing a hand on his shoulder. "It's for work. I know how frustrating this must be for you both."

Lucía shot Mom a furious look.

"Papi!" she yelled. "Sarah is trying to make us leave but we only just got here. Can't I stay with you for a bit?"

David ran his hand through his mop of black hair, his face drawn into an apologetic frown.

"Sorry, sweetheart," he said. "I have all these samples to analyze. Not today."

"This is *so unfair*," said Lucía. "All I want to do is solve a mystery."

Just then, the door to the zookeepers' area opened again. This time the frame was filled by a tall man, shaking his fist.

It was Victor.

"Which one of you took my roster?" Victor yelled.

Idris looked around the room, wondering why any one of them would take Victor's roster when there was already one pinned to the wall.

Maira shook her head. "What would we want with your roster, Victor?"

"I don't know and I don't care," Victor growled. "That roster had important information on it. I need to locate it immediately."

"Well, I don't think you will find it here," said Maira. "But you are welcome to look at ours if you like." She pointed to the wall where Lucía was standing.

Idris's gaze followed Maira's outstretched finger and landed on Lucía, whose eyes were sparkling with the excitement of finding a new clue.

"It's time for us to go," Mom whispered, pushing Idris ahead of her. "Come on, Lucía. We shouldn't be here."

"I think Sarah's right," said David. "This"—he pointed at Victor and Maira—"could get ugly."

Lucía groaned and stuffed her notebook back into her utility belt, then followed Idris down the corridor.

"See you tonight, David," said Mom, before rushing after them, bumping into a cleaner in her hurry to get out of the building.

"This wasn't really what I had in mind for our zoo trip," Lucía grumbled as they reached the parking lot and climbed back into the car. "We didn't even check the perimeter."

As the car pulled away, Lucía craned her neck out of the window, frantically scribbling down notes about the outside of the zoo. Idris picked up another book from the back of Mom's seat and started to read.

Before they had reached the main road, Idris had already lost himself in a book about the invertebrates of Indonesia. When Lucía poked him in the ribs, it took him a couple of seconds to remember where he was.

"Look out of the back window," she said. He turned to look behind them, but all he could see was a line of traffic.

"What?" he asked.

"Don't you see who it is?" Lucía said. Idris squinted but couldn't make out the face of the person in the car behind them.

"It's Victor," Lucía said. "He's following us."

Idris closed one eye and then the other but all he could see was a fuzzy gray windshield.

"I can't see a thing through that dirty windshield," he said. "But even if it *was* him, what possible reason could he have for following us?"

"I'm telling you," she said, "it's *him*." She scribbled something in her notebook.

"What are you writing?" Idris asked.

"Everything that I've noticed," she said. "The license plate, the color of the car, the clothes he's wearing. As a spy, it's important to be observant; you never know when this information might come in useful."

"Right," said Idris.

He let his gaze wander out of his side window and noticed that Mom was taking a wrong turn.

"It's not this way, Mom," he said. "You should have taken Beaconsfield Road."

"Ah yes," said Mom, "yes, you're right. My mistake."

Lucía raised her eyebrows dramatically. "Told you," she mouthed.

Idris shook his head. Mom was just forgetful; there was no reason to think anything else.

When they finally arrived home, Lucía and Idris raced up the stairs to the apartment.

"What are we going to do for the rest of the day?" asked Lucía. "I thought we would at least stay at the zoo for lunch."

"There are some pizzas in the freezer," said Mom. "And I'm sorry we had to leave the zoo. We'll do something really good this afternoon to make up for it."

The doorbell rang.

"That will be my package," said Mom. "Idris, just turn the oven on, would you, sweetheart? I'll run down and grab it."

After switching on the oven, Idris turned to find Lucía with her head buried in the fridge. She pulled out some bowls covered in plastic wrap.

"There are plenty of leftovers from last night," she said. "And there are a couple more avocados in the fridge. I'll make something much tastier than frozen pizza."

By the time lunch was ready, Mom still hadn't come back up to the apartment.

"That's weird," said Idris. "I wonder where Mom is. I think I'll go down and check."

When Idris got downstairs, he found the front door wide open and Mom nowhere to be seen. He ran to the car. It was locked and empty—exactly as they had left it. He raced back up to the apartment, pulled out his mobile phone, and dialed Mom's number.

"Is everything all right?" Lucía asked.

Something on the table started vibrating. It was Mom's bag. She had left her phone behind.

"No," said Idris. "Everything is *not* all right. **MOM IS GONE!**"

"What do you mean, she's gone?" said Lucía. "Gone where?"

"I don't know," said Idris. "But I'm sure she wouldn't have gone out on her own without saying goodbye. And she never goes anywhere without her bag and phone and they are both up here and she's not."

Lucía looked concerned.

"I'll ring Papi," she said, pulling out her own phone. Idris could hear it ring and ring until eventually going to voicemail. "No reply," Lucía said. "I'll leave a message."

Idris's breathing grew faster. "What

do we do?" he said. "Where could she possibly have gone?"

He paced up and down the kitchen until he remembered what Mom had said before they left.

"The emergency kit."

Both children looked up at the emergency kit, which sat high on top of the kitchen units.

"Leave it to me," said Lucía, cracking her knuckles and bouncing from foot to foot. "Spies need to be good at this kind of thing." Without taking off her shoes, she clambered up onto the work surface.

With one foot waggling wildly in the air and both arms outstretched, Lucía managed to grab the kit just in time, before her foot slipped and she came crashing to the kitchen floor.

The kit clattered open. Both children scrambled toward it, eager to see what it contained, but to their great surprise, it was empty. Next to Idris, a small scrap of paper floated to the ground.

"Was this inside the kit?" he asked.

Lucía chewed her lip. "Not sure. What does it say?"

Idris held the paper up to his face, turned it over, spun it around 360 degrees, and then held it out to Lucía.

"Nothing," he said. "It's blank."

"Blank?" Lucía asked. "But that makes no sense. What good is a blank piece of paper in an emergency?"

"I don't know," said Idris. "But this is crazy. I'm calling the police." He grabbed his phone and started to dial.

"Wait!" said Lucía, holding the paper to her nose and sniffing deeply. "Smell this."

"Smell it?"

Lucía nodded.

Idris leaned toward the paper and sniffed it tentatively. It smelled clean and vaguely citrusy.

"Well?" Lucía asked, tapping her foot impatiently.

Idris shook his head. "I don't smell anything."

Lucía growled.

"*Lemon!*" she said. "You know what *that* means, don't you."

Idris shook his head again.

"It's a secret message! Where is your iron?"

With all the emotion of Mom being missing and the discovery that the emergency kit was empty, Idris had had enough.

"Will you STOP with the spy stuff? You want an *iron?* My mom is MISSING, the emergency kit is empty, and we can't

get in touch with any grown-ups. This is not a game any more, Lucía. This is *bad*."

Lucía wasn't listening. She had run over to the oven, which was still switched on even though they had never put the pizzas inside it, and pressed the paper on the door.

"Are you even listening to me, Lucía?"

Idris's words were cut short. There, in front of his eyes, words were appearing on the paper.

"What's going on?" he asked.

"I told you!" Lucía grinned. "It's a hidden message! Sometimes, when spies want to send each other secret letters, they send each other what look like blank pieces of paper. But they are not blank at all! They are *hidden messages*. They contain all sorts of important information, you just have to figure out how to read them.

There are lots of different ways to hide or encode your messages—this message was written with invisible ink. There are many different types of invisible ink. One of them is lemon juice! You reveal the message by heating it up."

Idris was shocked beyond words. He leaned closer to see what the message said. He couldn't believe his eyes.

> In a true emergency,
> gain access to my secret study
> using the following code:
> 67ef4g5

"What does it mean?" Idris asked.

"It means I was right about your mom!" Lucía said. "I knew there was something funny about that burglar alarm..." She ran through to the hallway.

"Burglar alarm?" asked Idris. "What burglar alarm?"

Lucía stopped beside a plastic plaque mounted on the wall in the hallway and opened her utility belt.

"When I was exploring the apartment with my UV flashlight," she said, pulling out a small red flashlight, "I found that this plastic thing had letters and numbers written all over it in UV pen. I assumed it was a burglar alarm." She started pressing various parts of the plastic. "But now I realize it wasn't a burglar alarm at all." A green light flashed and there was a small beeping sound. "I think it's the entrance to a secret room!"

"I TOLD YOU SHE WAS A SPY!" yelled Lucía as the wall in front of them slid away, revealing a secret study between the bathroom and the master bedroom. The study's walls were covered in screens. One of these streamed a twenty-four-hour news channel, another held a picture of a purple sports car, and others were covered in maps and pictures. A large desk stood in the center. Idris was in too much shock to respond. "This is *amazing!*" Lucía said. She sank into a padded leather spinning chair. "Ooh, I could get used to this." She looked up at Idris. "You're looking a little green. Are you OK?"

XBA110
V2710·2478_901
_MC5029
2111063
EAKING... BREAKING... BRE
NEWS 24

He shook his head slowly. "I think I might throw up."

"Here," said Lucía, jumping out of the seat. "Sit down. It's just a shock. I'll go and get you a glass of water."

As he waited, Idris looked around the room. How was there a whole room in his apartment that he'd never known about? How had Mom kept this from him? Did this mean Lucía really was right? Was Mom *actually* a spy after all?

Lucía returned with two glasses of water and a packet of cookies.

"How are you feeling?" she asked, through a mouthful of cookie.

"I'm OK," said Idris, sipping gingerly from one of the glasses.

"Do you believe me now?" Lucía sprayed a fountain of crumbs around the room.

"Careful," said Idris, as the crumbs fell into an open drawer. "This stuff looks important."

He lifted a sheet of flamingo-pink paper to shake the crumbs onto the floor. His mind wandered to the paper he had seen in Mom's pocket last night during dinner. As he lifted the sheet, two words caught his eye: *Operation Pinecone*. Beneath the title was a message.

OPERATION PINECONE

Theft at Central Zoo.

Agent Maned Wolf will rendezvous

with Agent Walrus tomorrow for a

CODE RED KITE.

"Well, there you have it!" squealed Lucía. "She was investigating the pangolin theft!

That must be why she wanted to take us to the zoo. I wonder if she's Agent Walrus or Agent Maned Fox..."

"Why didn't she say something?" Idris wondered.

"Because she's not allowed to, is she? She's a spy!"

"A kidnapped spy," Idris reminded her. "Shall we tell the police now?"

"We can't tell the police!" said Lucía. "We could jeopardize the whole operation. She obviously gave us the code to the study because she wanted us to solve the mystery ourselves. What do you think a Code Red Kite is?"

Idris thought again about the man in the brown hat. Had that been Agent Walrus? He had certainly *looked* like a walrus, with his round face and droopy moustache.

If he *was* Agent Walrus, then did that make Mom Agent Maned Wolf? And what had Agent Walrus placed into Mom's pocket?

Idris took a deep breath and told Lucía about what he had seen. She let him finish before exploding.

"And you didn't think to tell me all this BEFORE?"

"I didn't think it was relevant," said Idris. "And I didn't really believe what I was seeing."

"Not relevant?" Lucía screamed. "You do know what you saw, don't you? That was a *brush contact*. Sarah—sorry, Agent Maned Wolf—showed she was ready for the contact by placing a *marker* on the board, Agent Walrus wiped his brow as a *signal* to let her know he was ready too, and then they brushed past each other as if they were strangers, allowing Agent Walrus to secretly drop something into Agent Maned Wolf's pocket without raising the alarm. That was *crucial information*, Idris. I can't believe you didn't tell me." She shook her head incredulously. "OK, think, Lucía, think. What could Agent Walrus have put into Agent Maned Wolf's pocket?"

Idris looked down at the papers in the drawer and his eyes fell on an iPad. On the screen an icon was flashing—it was a rusty-colored bird with long black-and-white wings.

"Red kite..." Idris whispered.

"What did you say?" Lucía asked.

Idris picked up the iPad and pointed at the flashing icon.

"This bird, it's a red kite."

"Amazing, Idris!" said Lucía. "Press it!"

Idris tapped the red kite symbol and a new screen opened. *Activate tracker?* it asked. The options were *Yes* or *No.*

"A tracker!" squealed Lucía. "That must be what Agent Walrus dropped into Agent Maned Wolf's pocket."

Idris looked at the screen again.

"Should I activate it?" he asked.

Lucía nodded eagerly.

"If Agent Maned Wolf still has the tracker in her pocket then it will show us exactly where she is!"

Idris selected *Yes.* A rotating circle told him something was loading, then a new message appeared on the screen.

Please open the app on your mobile device, it said.

"What do you think that means?" Idris said.

"It must be her phone," said Lucía. She ran out of the study before Idris could remind her that Mom didn't have a smartphone. As he entered the kitchen, Lucía was rummaging through his mom's bag. After a few moments she pulled out not one but two phones. One was Mom's usual flip phone, but the other was a smartphone—Idris had never seen it before.

"I don't know where this one came from," Idris said, taking the smartphone. He pressed the home button but he couldn't access it. "It's locked."

"Try her birthday," said Lucía. "Papi's birthday is his password for everything."

Idris typed in the numbers.

"Nope," he said. "Not that."

"Hmm," said Lucía. "Maybe try 12345?"

Idris shook his head. "Not that either. We only have one more try."

Lucía scratched her head. "Try your birthday?" she said.

He typed in the digits. The screen sprang to life.

"I'm in!"

Idris scrolled through the phone's various screens, until he came across a red kite icon. He opened it. *Tracking in progress,* the screen said, before opening a map, with a flashing blue dot moving across the page.

"There she is!" said Lucía. "The tracker must still be in her pocket. All we have to do is follow it..."

A knot pulled tightly in Idris's stomach.

He wasn't sure how he felt about chasing after Mom and her kidnappers. What would they do when they found her?

"Right now she's moving along..." Lucía squinted at the screen. "Beaconsfield Road."

"She's traveled pretty far already," said Idris. "Beaconsfield Road is the stop before my school."

"Then we better get going," said Lucía.

"How will we get there?" asked Idris.

"We will take the bus," said Lucía. "Like you do every day."

"Don't you think it's a bit dangerous?" asked Idris. "We can't just go chasing across the city in search of criminals."

"Of course we can," said Lucía. "We will take Philby just in case. She will protect us. And I will call Papi on the way to let him know where we are going."

She shoved Philby's leash into Idris's hand. Philby looked up at him with her crab toy in her mouth and wagged her tail gently.

Idris wasn't sure she would make much of a guard dog.

"Come on, we need to get going!"

"I'm really not sure about this," said Idris.

"We'll be fine," said Lucía, pointing at a pile of snacks, drinks, and dog treats. "Stick those in your backpack, would you? And do you have any books about pangolins?"

Idris paused to think for a moment. As Lucía pushed a screwdriver and her spy drone into the bag, he went to the bottom shelf of his bookcase. He found a book entitled *The Mammals of Southeast Asia.*

"Bring that too," Lucía said. "You never know, it might come in useful."

Ten minutes later they were waiting at the bus stop. Lucía tried to call her dad again, but again it went to voicemail. As Lucía left another message, Idris stared at the tracker. Suddenly, it stopped moving.

"Oh no," he said, tapping the screen of the phone.

"What's wrong?" mouthed Lucía, covering the microphone.

Idris pointed at the phone. "It's the tracker, I think it's lost signal."

"Hang on, Papi," said Lucía. "I will call you back in a minute." She snatched the phone. "What have you done?"

"Nothing," said Idris. "The dot just stopped moving. Look, it gives the last recorded location and the time."

He showed Lucía the screen.

"Great." She groaned. "Well, we'll just have to go to the last place it was recorded and hope we can find a clue."

It wasn't a long bus journey, but with his head full of worries about what may have happened to Mom, to Idris it seemed like an eternity.

"I wonder what else we can find in here," said Lucía, flicking through Mom's secret phone.

"I don't know if you should be snooping in there," Idris said.

"How else are we going to find clues that might help us save her?" snapped Lucía.

Idris didn't reply.

"Hey, look at this," Lucía said, holding the phone up for him to see.

It was a picture of printed sheet of paper.

"What's that?" Idris asked.

"Zoom in," said Lucía. He did. It was some kind of table, with dates and times in one column, names in the next column, and animal types in the final column.

"Do you remember when we were at the zoo?" said Lucía. "Victor was looking for his roster."

Idris nodded.

"This"—she tapped the screen excitedly—"is a picture of that roster! And look..." She zoomed in on one line in particular. "Who does it say was on duty the day the pangolins went missing?"

Idris scrolled across to read the name. The name "Gethin" had been typed into the box, but somebody had crossed it out and replaced it with a different one.

Idris drew in a loud breath. "Victor."

"Exactly. So that must be why he didn't want anyone to find his copy of the roster," said Lucía. "On the typed version, nobody would know that there had been a last-minute change of plan, but this hand-written version shows that *Victor* was the one that was responsible for the pangolins that day!"

"And if Mom had Victor's roster, maybe that's why he followed her—to get it back and destroy the evidence."

The bus came to a stop.

"This is where we get off," said Idris. "Come on, Philby." He waved a hand at the driver, mouthing "Thank you" as they clambered down the steps. "Which way now?"

Lucía opened the tracker map. She glanced from the screen to the street and back again several times.

"Up here and on the left," she said, pointing down the road. The two children and their dog scurried down the street until they came to a driveway with tall concrete pillars and a rusty metal gate. Down an overgrown driveway, they could just make out a small white cottage, with a red car parked outside.

Lucía looked up from the phone and gave a little squeak.

"That's the car that was following us home from the zoo, I'm sure of it!" She handed the phone to Idris and ferreted around in her utility belt before pulling out the notebook to compare the license plates. "Yes, it is! Idris, we must be in the right place."

Idris's stomach turned a somersault.

Lucía pushed open the rusty gate. It gave a loud ***kerrrreak***.

"**Shhh**," whispered Idris, "someone will hear you."

They crept quietly up the driveway, leaving the gate open behind them. The hedges, though very prickly, provided the perfect cover for creeping toward the cottage unseen.

"What are we going to do when we get there?" whispered Idris. "Have you thought about that?"

Lucía turned, her eyes wide and one finger pushed hard against her lips. "**Shhh**" She jabbed a finger toward the front door. It was opening. Idris flung himself to the floor, rolling under the hedge. Next to him, Lucía did the same, with Philby held tight under one of her arms. They peered through the leaves as a figure walked out onto the doorstep.

Beside Lucía, Philby rustled in the bushes. Idris covered his mouth to stop himself from squealing. The person turned in the direction of the sound and Idris pushed his face into the ground. But not before getting a good look at the man's large, beak-like nose, turned-out feet, and hunched, vulture-like posture. There was no doubt about it. It was Victor.

Idris held his breath, hoping they wouldn't be seen. After scanning the bushes for a couple of seconds, Victor walked down the steps, climbed into the car, and started the engine. After a couple of engine splutters, a big cloud of black smoke billowed out of the exhaust and he reversed up and out of the driveway.

"Did you see that?" Idris asked. Lucía nodded.

"I *knew* it was him!" Lucía said breathlessly. She scrambled out from underneath the bushes, her hair full of twigs and leaves. "Quick, let's go and take a look around his house while he's gone."

She scurried toward the front door, dragging Philby along beside her, and tried the handle.

"It's locked," she said.

"Shall we go and see if there's a back door?" asked Idris.

"Good idea," said Lucía. "You do that and I will see if I can find an open window."

Idris walked around the outside of the house, his heart thundering in his chest.

He came to a small courtyard, where a pair of patio doors led into Victor's kitchen. He tried the handle. It was locked.

He thought about what Mom told him

to do whenever he had lost something; "do a systematic search, Idris—and don't forget the obvious!"

But where would be an obvious place to hide a key? Idris glanced around the courtyard and noticed some flower pots on either side of the door. One by one, he lifted them, eyes scanning the floor for anything unusual. But there was nothing to be seen. *Not that obvious,* Idris thought. Ok, systematic search, where else could Victor have hidden a key? He spotted some small, smooth stones at the base of a brick wall. Under those, perhaps? He lifted each of them in turn. The first two were unremarkable, normal stones with nothing beneath. Then he lifted the third. Something about this stone felt different. Instead of being dense and heavy, it felt light and hollow. Not at all the way a stone should feel. He gave the stone a shake—what was that? Something was jangling inside! Idris worked his fingers around the outside of the stone until he found a small, barely noticeable recess. As his thumb slipped into the recess, a crack appeared, then the edge of the stone gave way, revealing a small hidden plate. Idris gasped. Inside was a key.

"Lucía!" he shouted. "Lucía, come here, I've found something!"

In a flash, Lucía and Philby appeared beside him. Lucía was breathing heavily.

"How did you find that?" Lucía asked.

Idris shook his head. "I just did a systematic search."

Lucía gave him an approving look.

"You know," she said, "I think you could

be quite good at this spying thing if you wanted to."

"I don't want to," said Idris. "I just want to get Mom back and then I never want to hear the word '**spy**' again."

"Go on, then," Lucía said. "What are you waiting for? Put the key in the lock."

Idris tried to move his arm toward the door but found that he was frozen to the spot; he was too frightened about what they would find inside to move. Lucía grabbed the key from his hand and put it into the lock. She gave it a jiggle and then they heard a loud ***click.***

Lucía looked back at him, her face flushed with excitement.

"It worked!" she whispered. She pushed down the door handle and the door swung toward them.

From inside the room, a foul smell burst out and engulfed them. This seemed to break whatever spell had been holding Idris there and he jumped back, coughing.

The kitchen smelled absolutely terrible. What had happened in there? As they entered, Idris eyed a table that had fallen on its side, books strewn about the floor, and wooden pellets littered across the pale gray tiles. At the far end of the room was a sofa, which had three large scratches across it. It looked as if there had been some kind of struggle.

"Looks like a tiger has been let loose in here," said Lucía. "What do you think made those marks?" She was pointing at the sofa.

Idris frowned. An image of a pangolin floated into his mind, its powerful front legs ending in long, curved claws.

"Pangolins have big claws," Idris said. "Three on each of their front feet."

"You think a cute little pangolin did this?" said Lucía. "I thought you said they were gentle?"

Idris shrugged. "They wouldn't hurt a person but pangolins feed on ants and termites. They use their strong front feet to break into ants' nests and termite mounds. So if a pangolin was hungry and it thought there might be termites inside that sofa..."

"Gosh," said Lucía. "Well, anyway, whatever caused those scratches definitely shouldn't be here, and that means Victor is up to no good."

Idris swallowed nervously. And what about his mom? Did that mean she was here too?

"**Mom?**" Idris shouted. "Mom are you here?"

There was a noise from the next room.

"**MOM!**" he shouted. "It's ok, I'm coming!"

He ran to a wooden door behind the sofa and heaved it open. On the other side of the door was a small room. It was very dark.

"Mom?" he said, uncertainly. "Are you there?"

Lucía pushed past Idris and flicked a switch on the wall. A bright light flickered, illuminating everything in its warm glow. The room was cluttered with boxes of animal feed, plastic bowls, and rubber boots.

Suddenly, Idris and Lucía heard a growl.

Idris turned, wide-eyed, to Lucía. At his feet, Philby gave a little whimper.

"Did you hear that?" he whispered.

Lucía nodded.

"What do you think it was?"

Lucía didn't have a chance to answer because a voice spoke from the far corner of the room. A voice with which Idris was very familiar.

"Hello children, you took your time."

Idris spun around to see a woman in a flowery dress, arms and legs bound with string, sitting quietly on a plastic chair in the corner.

"**Mom!**" shouted Idris. "You're all right!"

He rushed over to her, trying not to trip over the boxes, and wrapped his mom in an enormous hug. His heart felt like it might burst with relief. Lucía gave Mom a quick hug too, then the children both set about undoing Mom's bindings, desperate to get her free before Victor returned. They had just about released her when Philby gave a short, sharp bark.

Idris looked up to see a tall man standing in the doorway, a shopping bag in one hand and a deep scratch on the other.

Victor had returned.

"Who do we have here?" Victor said, stepping into the room.

"When did he get back?" Lucía whispered. "You could have warned us earlier, Philby!" Philby wagged her tail at the sound of her voice and gave Lucía's leg a lick.

Victor moved closer. "I think it's time we all had a little chat," he said.

Idris stepped in front of Mom, lifting his fists in front of his face protectively.

"If you want to hurt my mom, you're going to have to get through me first."

Philby gave out a little woof.

Victor scowled.

"I don't want to hurt your mom, Idris. Or you or your dog for that matter. Please, take a seat. All I want to do is explain myself."

Idris looked nervously from Mom to Lucía to Victor.

"It's OK, Idris," said Mom calmly. "Let Victor speak."

Idris lowered his hands.

"OK," he said. "But one wrong move..."

"Thank you, Idris," said Victor, taking a deep breath. "I can see how all this must look."

"Like you kidnapped Idris's mom and tied her up in your utility room?" Lucía said.

Victor paused to swallow. "Yes, I suppose that's exactly how it looks. I'm sorry, Idris. You must have been awfully worried about your mom." He gave a little murmur and sank to the floor.

"Really worried," said Idris with a frown. This wasn't the direction he had imagined this conversation would go in.

"Oh dear," Victor said. He let out a ragged breath and to Idris's great surprise, looked like he might be about to cry. "I never meant for any of this to happen," he said, wiping away a tear with the back of one of his large hands. "It just all started to spiral out of control and then..."

"Start from the beginning," said Mom kindly. "Nobody is judging you; we just want to hear what you have to say."

Idris and Lucía shared a look. Mom might not be judging Victor, but they definitely were.

"All right," said Victor. "You're very kind. I don't deserve your kindness after the way I've treated you." He hiccupped. "But I do owe you an explanation, so here goes..." He cleared his throat and then fixed them all with an earnest gaze. "On the day of the theft of the pangolins, Gethin was on duty but sadly, he had a family emergency and I was drafted in to help at the last minute. I was due to do a check between 4 and 5 p.m. Unfortunately, earlier that day, David—your dad, Lucía—had come to me and told me that one of the lion cubs had been rejected by its mother and needed to be hand-reared—"

Victor lifted a blanket to reveal a large metal crate, right next to Mom's chair. Inside the crate was a small, furry, sleeping lion cub!

"Moshi!" said Lucía and Idris.

"Yes," said Victor, "that's right, how did you...? Anyway, of course I offered to help with Moshi. We brought him back here, made him a nice bed, gave him his medication, and before I knew it, it was 6 p.m. I had totally forgotten to go and feed the pangolins. By the time I got to the zoo it was too late: the police were there and the pangolins had already been taken."

In any other scenario, Idris would have had a million questions about the lion cub, but right now there were too many other things to think about.

"You were with my dad the whole time the theft was taking place?" Lucía asked, looking confused.

Victor nodded.

"Moshi took a little bit of settling in," Victor said. "And he wasn't hugely happy about taking his medication."

"That explains the scratches on your face," said Idris.

"And the sofa," said Lucía.

"And the growling," said Mom.

But it still didn't explain why Victor had kidnapped Mom.

"If you had an alibi then why didn't you just explain that you had forgotten?" asked Idris.

Victor hung his head sadly.

"I was embarrassed, Idris," he said. "I have never forgotten to feed the animals before. And I can't lose this job. It's my everything. I've worked at the zoo my whole life; I don't know what I would do without it."

"But you were busy looking after Moshi," said Idris. "You had nothing to be ashamed of. Nobody would have blamed you! Until you kidnapped my mom, that is."

Victor grimaced.

"Yes, that was a big mistake," he said. "When I saw the folded-up roster in her bag at the zoo I panicked. I thought that she would turn me in. Before I could think about what I was doing, I found myself following you all home. I didn't mean to hurt you, ma'am. I just wanted you to know that it wasn't me that stole the pangolins. I wanted a chance to explain. I would have told you before," he said. "But I wanted to go and get you some chocolate to apologize first." He pulled a red box out of the shopping bag and held it out to Mom.

For the first time since Victor's confession, Idris looked at Mom. She was smiling.

"Ooh, thank you, Victor. My favorites." She opened the top of the box. "I think we could all use some chocolate, couldn't we?" She tapped a label on the side of the box. "Don't worry, Idris. Palm oil free!"

She handed the chocolates around.

"You're not angry?" Idris asked. "He just kidnapped you and tied you up."

Mom laughed.

"It's not the first time I've been kidnapped," Mom said, with a wink. "Victor didn't hurt me and he's already apologized. Though it was all a bit unnecessary, Victor. I always knew you didn't take the pangolins."

"You did?" said Victor, Idris, and Lucía in unison.

"I did!" Mom smiled.

"If Victor didn't take the pangolins," said Idris, "then who did?"

"I believe it was someone called the Countess," said Mom, biting into a chocolate. "We have been investigating her for some time. My suspicions were all but confirmed when I spotted her dressed as a cleaner at the zoo this morning."

"At the zoo *this morning?*" said Idris. "Why didn't you arrest her there and then?"

"Well, for a start I don't have the power to arrest people." Mom laughed. "And secondly, we don't have any evidence that it was her yet, just a hunch."

"If you thought you saw her this

morning," interrupted Lucía, "then why didn't you place the tracker on her?"

"I did," said Mom. "Did you notice that I bumped into a cleaner as we were leaving? That was no accident. I dropped the tracker into her pocket."

"But that makes no sense," said Idris. "We activated the tracker and followed it. We thought it was still in your pocket. It brought us straight here, to you..."

"It did?" said Mom, looking concerned.

"Actually, technically," said Lucía, passing Mom the smartphone, "it lost signal here. We just assumed that if we followed the tracker to its last location we would find a clue about where you could be."

Idris quickly explained how they had decoded the secret message in the emergency kit, accessed Mom's study, and unlocked the tracker app before following its signal to find her in Victor's house.

"I'm very proud of you both," said Mom. "That was some excellent spycraft. I still don't understand why the tracker I put on the Countess led you here though..."

"Let me get this straight," said Idris. "You're telling me we were tracking the *Countess,* a dangerous animal-stealing criminal, instead of you this *whole time?*"

"You were!" said Mom. "Excellent work. I'm very grateful for your help."

Idris felt a little bit sick. What if they had found the Countess instead of Mom? Thank goodness the tracker had lost signal before they had caught up with her.

"What would make a tracker lose signal?" Lucía asked.

"Hmm," pondered Mom. "It shouldn't have run out of battery because it is brand new. I suppose it could have been damaged in some way. Trackers also lose signal if you go underground, but that seems unlikely around here—"

Victor raised his hand.

"Do you mind if I interrupt?" he asked.

"Sure," said Mom. "What is it?"

"Well, actually, it *is* possible that the Countess went underground here. Just behind my house you can access the old postal tunnels."

"Postal tunnels?" asked Idris. "What are they?"

"A network of underground tunnels," said Victor. "They lead right under the zoo. I use them to get to work every day!"

"I think you're right," said Mom, holding

up the phone. "The tracker has just found signal again—and look where she is!"

Victor took the phone and zoomed in on the map.

"She's back at the zoo," he said, "in the Southeast Asia house."

"Do you think she is going to try to steal some more animals?" Idris asked.

"There's only one way to find out," said Mom. "Victor, take us to the postal tunnels!"

At that moment, Lucía's phone started to ring. The four of them looked down at the screen.

Papi.

"What am I going to tell him?" asked Lucía. "He's going to be so worried."

"Don't tell him any of this just yet," said Mom. "Tell him we couldn't find Philby, but that we have found her now and she's fine and there's no need for him to worry."

Lucía nodded.

"*Hola*, Papi," she said. "Yes, I know, I'm so sorry to have worried you, it's just we lost Philby. Yes, yes, she's fine now, don't worry.

Yes, we're all fine. Idris and Sarah too. Yes, you do sound very busy. No need to worry about us..."

As Lucía was speaking to her dad, an idea popped into Idris's head. He waved at her frantically as she was saying goodbye.

"Oh, wait a minute, Papi, I think Idris wants to speak to you."

She passed him the phone.

"Hi, David," said Idris. "I was just wondering if you had managed to put that camera in the orangutan enclosure yet?"

"Yes, we put it in at twelve o'clock," David replied. "As soon as the visitors left. Why do you ask?"

"Just wondered if you had seen anything interesting on the footage yet?" said Idris.

"I haven't had a chance to check it,"

said David. "I've been running all these samples and Maira has had to rush off elsewhere. The camera will have to wait until later. Great idea, though—thanks, Idris. Now I really have to get back to work, otherwise I won't be home in time for dinner."

David hung up.

"Did he suspect anything?" asked Mom.

Lucía shook her head. "I don't think so. It didn't feel right, though, lying to him."

"Don't worry," said Idris. "I think he's more worried about all those samples he has to run. He hasn't even had a chance to look at the footage from the camera in the orangutan enclosure yet."

"Which camera have they used?" asked Victor.

"They said it was the one they had used for the lioness," said Idris.

"If it's the same video feed from Zahara's enclosure," said Victor, "then I should have access to the live weblink. I was the one who kept an eye on her to see when she had her babies."

He pulled out a grubby laptop, wiped away a layer of golden animal hairs, then started pressing buttons. The orangutan enclosure crackled into focus. Budi was huddled in a corner.

"Oh, Budi," said Idris.

"Does it have sound?" Mom asked. Victor fiddled with some buttons on the keyboard and a crackling sound emerged from the speakers.

"What's that?" said Lucía, pointing to a patch of shrubbery in the middle of the screen. To their surprise, the bush shook a little then rose clean into the air.

"Is that normal?" Lucía asked Victor.

He shook his head. "Absolutely not normal."

Shortly after, a person emerged from beneath the plant.

"It's a trapdoor!" said Mom.

"It's the cleaner I bumped into this

morning," said Idris.

"That's no cleaner," Mom said.

Idris and Lucía looked at each other, open-mouthed.

"It's the Countess!"

"Shh," said Mom. "She's saying something."

"I won't be bothering you for much longer," the Countess said to Budi. "Everything is ready. The pangolins are packed away in the warehouse, ready to make me rich!"

She rubbed her hands together hungrily.

"As soon as the zookeeper on duty has done his checks, I will zoom around in my car and scoop the little beasts up. Then I will be out of your hair forever!"

She pulled a jangling set of keys from her belt.

"So long, monkey." Then she let herself out of the orangutan enclosure and disappeared from view. Budi remained huddled in the corner, pushing himself as far away from the intruder as possible. No wonder he was out of sorts. His enclosure was being used as an animal trafficking highway.

"Poor Budi," said Idris. "He looked terrified. *And* she called him a monkey."

"We still have time to save the pangolins," said Lucía. "When do the zookeepers leave?"

Victor looked at his watch. "Twenty-five minutes."

"Then there's no time to lose," said Mom. "We need to get to the zoo, fast! Can you take us in your car, Victor?"

Victor shook his head. "Afraid not,"

he said. "Moshi is due some more medicine in ten minutes; besides, it's quicker to use the tunnels. I will show you the entrance."

He led them out of the house and through his back yard to a stone archway nestled within the trees. He pulled open the round wooden door and ushered them inside.

"Down there," he said.

Idris glanced nervously at Lucía, who didn't seem to share his concern.

"Exciting!" she said. "Now this is what I call an adventure!"

Chapter Twelve

The tunnel was dark and foreboding. Its gray stone walls were covered in lime-green moss and smelled of damp and mold. As they climbed inside, a cold droplet of water plopped onto the back of Idris's neck, sending a shiver down his spine.

Everything about this tunnel matched

his mood perfectly. He felt miserable. Everything he thought he knew had been a lie. Now he was following his mom—who was in fact a spy—down a gloomy tunnel in search of an international criminal. **Not your average Wednesday.**

As he watched Mom clambering deftly down the tunnel, he thought about all of the adventures they could have had together if only he had known the truth.

"Are you all right, Idris?" Mom asked. "I recognize that face. You're worried."

He shrugged.

"You sure know a lot about me, don't you?" he said. "That must be nice. I know nothing about you any more. Everything you have told me has been a lie."

Mom didn't reply. Idris clenched his fists. Anger and sadness bubbled inside him.

"Was any of it real?" he asked. "What about the factory? Do you actually work there or was that all just a made-up story too?"

Idris slowed to a halt but Mom didn't realize and kept walking.

"What else is fake?" he shouted after her. "Is your name even Sarah?"

Mom turned and looked at him.

"Oh, Idris," she said. She walked back toward him, arms extended for a hug. He pushed her hands away.

"How do I know if I'm even your son?"

Mom looked really hurt by that last comment and Idris felt a little guilty. He didn't really believe she would lie about something as important as that.

"Idris," Mom said, speaking slowly and softly. "I'm sorry. I really am. Truly sorry that I've hurt you and really sorry that you found out like this. I only kept it from you to protect you."

"Great job you did of that," Idris grumbled, wiping his tears with the back of his hand.

"You're right," Mom said. "You've proved me wrong. You are brave and capable and I shouldn't have lied to you. But Idris, you have to know this: it was just my real job that I kept from you. My love for you was never a lie. The memories we have shared over all of these years—none of that was pretend. That is all real.

Our love is the most real thing in the world. You are my son and I love you." She reached out toward him and cupped his face between her hands, looking him right in the eyes. "The job that I have, the name that I'm given, the place that we live in—that can all change. But our truth, Idris..." She put her hand on his heart. "Our truth, that I will love you always and forever—that won't change. Not ever."

Something squirmed in Idris's stomach. He didn't know how to feel. He couldn't forgive Mom that easily for all the lies but at the same time he knew that what she said was true. The fact that she was a spy didn't change any of the important things, not really.

Luckily, he didn't have to respond,

for at that moment, the echo of Philby's barks came bouncing down the tunnel.

"You have to come down here!" Lucía shouted. "I think I've found something important!"

Idris and Mom broke into a run. Ahead of them they saw Lucía staring into a large crate.

Inside the crate were several drawstring sacks and a plastic tub that said *pangolin food*.

"The Countess must have stored the pangolins here before moving them to the warehouse," Mom said.

While Mom and Lucía looked inside the crate for more clues, Idris was distracted by Philby, who was sniffing the floor excitedly.

"What is it, Philbs?" Idris said. "Can you smell something?"

She looked up at him over her crab toy, wagged her tail and pulled on the leash, stretching to sniff the air farther down the tunnel.

"I think Philby is on the scent of something," said Idris. "Maybe we should follow her."

"This isn't one of your dog-training classes," Mom said. "You can't just tell Philby to fetch the pangolin. She's never seen one before. Besides, she can probably smell a rat. There will be loads of those down here. Just try to hold her still."

Idris covered Philby's ears.

"Don't listen to her," he said, whispering under his hand directly into Philby's ear. "I know you're good at finding things. We've been working hard on that."

Philby might not be any good at walking to heel or coming back when she was called, but she was an absolute genius at retrieving toys by name. In fact, she had learned the names of *ten* different objects and could reliably retrieve them whenever he asked. He had even taught her to deliver the objects to family members by name. A particular favorite had been when he had told her to fetch his socks and give them to Mom, and she had dropped Idris's stinky school socks right into Mom's oatmeal.

"Maybe we should ring Papi," Lucía said, looking concerned. "He might be starting to worry."

"Lucía," said Mom, very serious all of a sudden. "I know it's a lot to take in but it's very important that you keep my real job a secret. You can't tell your dad about any of this. He can't know about the investigation, or any of what you two have discovered. Nobody can."

Lucía tipped her head to one side, a curious expression on her face.

"What do you mean, I can't tell him?" she said. "I tell him everything."

"Well, you can't tell him this," Mom said. "It's too big a risk."

"He won't tell anyone," said Lucía. "We can't keep this from him. It's not fair!"

Mom sighed.

"Do you remember last year," Mom said, "when your dad arranged a surprise party for my birthday?"

Lucía and Idris nodded. It had been the most wonderful day. The Garcías were the best at throwing parties. Not so good at keeping secrets, though. Three weeks before the event, despite the fact that the whole party was meant to be a surprise, David had told Sarah all about it. Mom had still acted surprised when everyone had jumped out, but Idris and Lucía had known it was just an act.

"I suppose he's not the best secret-keeper," said Lucía reluctantly.

"Right. He's *the worst,*" Mom agreed. "Now imagine that secret could have put him in danger if he had told someone about it. Or, worse, put *you* in danger, Lucía. He would never forgive himself."

Lucía sniffed, then rubbed her nose vigorously on the back of her hand. "I guess you're right. I don't like it though."

"I know," said Mom. "It's hard being a spy. Sometimes we have to hide things from the people we love the most."

She glanced at Idris. His stomach squirmed again.

"All right," he said, changing the subject. "So how are we going to find these pangolins?"

Mom sighed. "I'm afraid it's going to be a good old-fashioned search. The Countess said she had moved the pangolins to a warehouse and we know from the tracker that she hasn't left these tunnels, so the warehouse must be down here somewhere."

"Maybe we should split up?" Idris suggested. "We would cover a greater area more quickly if we did that."

"But then what if we lose each other?" said Mom.

"I know," said Lucía. "What if I use my spy drone to scout out a couple of tunnels while you two head down that one?" She pointed down a tunnel to their right. "Then we can meet back here and report our findings."

"Sounds like a plan," said Mom. "Come on, Idris, let's go."

A few minutes later, halfway down the tunnel, Mom and Idris came across a ladder. It led right to the roof of the tunnel, where there was a trapdoor.

"Shall we?" asked Mom, indicating the ladder with her eyes. Idris nodded.

Mom went up first and Idris followed gingerly. She reached the top and opened the trapdoor, then gave out a little "**ooh**" of surprise. What could she have found? As Idris reached the final rungs of the ladder, his head popped into a bright and leafy room and he came face to face with the flanged, orange face of a startled male orangutan. They were inside Budi's enclosure!

"Budi!" said Idris. "You weren't the person we were looking for, but it's very nice to see you! How are you feeling today?"

Idris glanced around at the uneaten pile of fruit—whole melons, bananas, chunks of pineapple. Budi had barely touched it. "Still not great, hey? Well, I'm really sorry to be interrupting you again. You must be sick of people coming in and out but I have a feeling you're going to be feeling much better really soon. Just you wait."

Idris could have stayed and talked to Budi all day, but he was drawn away by sounds from below. Lucía was shouting. As Idris clambered back down the ladder, he started to be able to make out what Lucía was saying. Her words made his skin tingle.

"I've found it! I've found it! Idris, Sarah, hurry! I know just where we need to go."

Chapter Thirteen

Lucía was right. When Idris and Mom made it back to the fork in the tunnel, Lucía excitedly explained that she had found the warehouse using her spy drone. Together, the three of them hurried down a series of tunnels that eventually brought them to the warehouse. It was a large, gray room, with open garage doors at each end. Lucía had even been able to pinpoint the exact spot where the drawstring sack would be found before they reached it.

Idris pulled open the sack. Inside was a scaly ball, about the size of a soccer ball. Without considering whether it was the right thing to do, he reached into the bag and pulled the pangolin out.

"Wow," said Lucía.

The pangolin's scales were smooth and cool. It wasn't moving at all. In a flash of panic, Idris wondered if it might be dead—it had been kept overnight in a bag in a warehouse, after all. Then he saw its eye. Black as night and twinkling with the brilliance of a thousand stars, it stared up at him, wide and unblinking. It was alive.

"You're okay," he whispered, holding the pangolin tight to his chest. "You're safe now."

"Are they breathing?" Lucía asked.

"This one is," said Idris. "Get the other one out—it's in that sack."

Lucía reached into the sack and pulled out another scaly ball. Its tail was pulled tightly over its head but from beneath its scales, Idris could see its nostrils twitching.

"I can feel it moving," Lucía said, holding it up to her eyes. It lifted its head, which made Lucía squeak with fright. "Will it bite me?" she squealed, thrusting it away from her face.

Idris laughed.

"No," he said, "they don't have any teeth."

The pangolin sniffed the air, then uncurled

itself, clinging onto Lucía's arm for support.

"Hello, little friend," said Lucía. She was beaming.

"Yours is a lot braver than mine!" Idris laughed.

"It's so strong," Lucía said, trying to stop it from clambering up onto her shoulder. "Look at it go!"

"Right," said Mom. "Time is ticking. The Countess will be back soon and if she sees us here, she will suspect something; that could jeopardize the whole operation. Let's put the pangolins back in the sack and get in position."

"In position for what?" said Idris.

"To take pictures of the Countess stealing the pangolins," said Mom. She whipped out her smartphone and snapped a couple of pictures of the pangolins. "This is exactly the kind of evidence we need to arrest her."

"You mean we are not going to take the pangolins away with us?" Idris asked.

Mom glanced nervously at the pangolin in his hand.

"Not yet..." she said. "The Countess has to actually *take* the pangolins and sell them in order to be arrested for animal trafficking."

"But what if the pangolins get hurt on the way?" said Idris.

"She doesn't want to hurt them," Mom replied. "All the Countess cares about is money—and the pangolins are worth more alive than dead."

"What if we don't manage to rescue them before she sells them? Then if something awful happens to them it would be *our* fault."

"I suppose it would," said Mom.

Lucía chewed her lip thoughtfully.

"What if there was a way we could trick the Countess into thinking she *was* taking the pangolins?" said Lucía. "We could leave something in the bag that *felt* like pangolins instead."

"Taking a bag of pretend pangolins isn't a crime," said Mom.

"We can't let the Countess hurt these pangolins just so we can arrest her," said Idris. "It's not fair!"

"What about if we promised to find a way to help you arrest the Countess later," said Lucía. "Without any animals getting hurt."

"We've already proved we have what it takes to complete our own spy missions," Idris added.

"Ok...," said Mom. "I suppose that could work. And any pictures I take of her may help to build a case, even if she only *thinks* she's taking pangolins. But what could we put in their place? I don't suppose you have a pair of stunt pangolins in your pockets."

Idris thought back to the fruit he had seen strewn around Budi's cage.

"What about melons?" he said. "Melons and pineapples... I saw both of those in the orangutan enclosure."

Lucía considered the weight of the pangolin on her arm.

"A melon would be about right," she said.

"We could wrap the melons in the skin of the pineapples to give the impression of scales," Idris explained. "It won't be perfect. But it might convince her if she's in a hurry."

"There's no way that the Countess has any idea what a sack of pangolins feels like," said Lucía. "She's far more interested in how much money they can make her."

"I suppose it could work," said Mom. "But there isn't a lot of time left."

"Me and Idris can run back to Budi's enclosure and get the fruit," said Lucía. "While you hide behind those shelves with the pangolins. We will leave the fake pangolins here—" she marked the spot with Philby's crab toy. "And you will be in the perfect position to take pictures of the Countess stealing the bag."

"Sounds like a plan," said Mom.

Idris's palms started to sweat.

"What if we're not fast enough?" he said.

"We will be," said Lucía. "We have to be."

Mom pulled them both in for a hug.

"You're more capable than you think," she whispered. "You already tracked down a spy and rescued her!"

Idris smiled.

"Come on, Philby," he said, pulling on her leash and walking quickly away, causing her to drop her crab toy. "One last adventure."

Philby barked and pulled at her leash as she tried to pick up her toy again but Idris pulled her away.

"Leave it," he said. "We will be back soon."

As he left the warehouse, Idris turned to see Mom clambering behind the shelves, the sack of pangolins clutched tightly in her fist.

I hope this works, he thought.

Idris, Lucía, and Philby quickly retraced their steps, finding themselves back at the bottom of the ladder in record time.

This time, when Idris popped up into the enclosure, Budi was taking a nap.

"Hello, Budi," Idris smiled. "So sorry to burst in on you *again*. I just need to borrow a couple of melons. I hope you don't mind."

Budi, who had opened one eye when Idris appeared, shut it again without making a sound.

Idris heaved himself into the enclosure and hurried over to a pile of fruit, scooping up two large melons as well as a half-eaten pineapple.

"Thanks, Budi," Idris murmured, glancing over at the sleeping ape, who was now snoring loudly. "We won't bother you any more." He pulled the trap door closed and clambered back down the ladder.

"Well done!" said Lucía, taking a melon. "It's exactly the right weight!"

"Now we need to figure out a way to wrap the pineapple skin around the melons," said Idris. "So they don't feel so smooth." He wrapped the pineapple skin around the edge of the melon and rubbed his fingers over the surface. It felt surprisingly similar to the pangolins.

"Could these help?" asked Lucía, pulling a handful of paperclips from her utility belt. Idris took a couple, bending them so that he could push the sharp ends into the melon's skin. They held the pineapple skin on perfectly.

"They're great!" said Idris.

Just then, Philby started barking. From farther along the tunnel came a growling noise, which was steadily growing louder.

"McLaren 570GT," said Lucía, her eyes widening. "It must be the Countess! We need to get back to the warehouse *right now*. Quick, put the pangolin-melons back in here."

Lucía opened the drawstring sack and Idris dropped the pineapple-covered melons inside. Would they be back in time to convince the Countess? What would happen if they weren't? Would she find the real pangolins? What would happen if the Countess found Mom? Idris felt panic rise inside him. Philby, sensing his upset, pushed up against him. Suddenly, Idris had an idea.

"Come on, Idris, we need to go," said Lucía, hopping up and down.

"We're not fast enough," said Idris. "We'll never get there in time. But I know someone who is…" He looked pointedly at Philby.

"You want to give the sack to *Philby?*" Lucía said.

"I know it sounds crazy," said Idris. "But I trust her. We've been working really hard on her training. And you and me will never get there in time."

"OK," said Lucía hesitantly. Idris could see that her eyes were wide with worry. "What do you want to do?"

"Do you remember the trick I taught Philby, where I tell her to take her toy to someone?"

Lucía nodded.

"Well, we left her crab toy back in the warehouse, right in the place we wanted to put the pangolins. If she's smart enough to take a toy and give it to a person, I'm sure she's smart enough to take a toy and place it on top of another toy too."

"Have you ever done that trick with her before?" Lucía asked.

"Well, no," admitted Idris. "But I believe she can do it."

"It's a big risk," said Lucía.

"I know." Idris nodded. "But I trust her." He kneeled down next to Philby. "OK, Philbs," he said. "I have a really, really important job for you." He took a deep breath and held out the sack for Philby to sniff. "It's a little different than what we've done before, but I'm sure you'll figure it out."

Philby's tail whirred like a helicopter propeller. She knew what Idris was about to ask of her. It was her absolute favorite game. "Fetch sack," Idris said, passing her the sack containing the pineapple-melons. Philby took the sack in her jaws with a little yelp of excitement, waiting for the final part of the command. "Take to crab," Idris said. Philby cocked her head to one side and for a moment, Idris thought she might refuse to leave. He repeated the command and gave her a pat on the shoulder. Philby started wagging her tail again, gave another little yelp and then turned in a tight circle before galloping off down the tunnel.

When Idris looked around at Lucía, she looked pale.

"Do you think she understood what you said?"

"Yes," Idris said, with more confidence than he felt. "She's a smart dog and this trick is the one thing she can do really, really well."

"I hope you're right," said Lucía. "Come on, let's go."

She raced off down the tunnel, with Idris

trailing close behind. The noises of the sports car grew louder and louder before stopping completely. Moments later, there came a loud shout.

"WHAT ARE YOU DOING WITH MY SACK, YOU FILTHY MUTT?"

"I think Philby has arrived in the warehouse," puffed Lucía.

Idris grimaced. "I hope the Countess doesn't hurt her."

They turned the corner into the warehouse, where a large purple car was parked between the open doors. They were just in time to see a woman bend to snatch at the bag in Philby's jaws. Philby gave a quiet, warning growl.

"Let go," snarled the woman, her purple hair slipping over her shoulders as she attempted to tug the bag from Philby's

mouth. But Philby would not let go.

"Should we do something?" whispered Idris.

"I'm not sure," replied Lucía. "Didn't your mom say it would jeopardize the whole operation if she saw us?"

The Countess took another step toward Philby, accidentally stepping on the crab toy. It gave a loud squeak, which echoed around the warehouse. At the sound of her favorite toy, Philby let go of the bag and grabbed the crab instead. Idris let out a sigh of relief. The first stage had been a success—now they had to hope the Countess didn't realize they had swapped the pangolins for melons.

The Countess brushed off the outside of the drawstring sack.

"You've covered it in slobber, you mangy stray," she said, before lifting the bag above her head and poking at its contents with her free hand. Her long index finger jabbed again and again at the drawstring sack, her sharp fingernails making a scratching noise against the coarse fabric. Idris's stomach lurched. They hadn't had time to prepare the fake pangolins properly. Had Philby jolted the bag and caused the pieces of fruit to come apart? What would happen if the Countess opened the bag now and saw a handful of pineapples and melons instead of her prized pangolins? He held his breath, not daring to imagine. After a final prod, the Countess stopped and looked at Philby, who was staring expectantly back at her. "What are you looking at?" the Countess growled.

Philby wagged her tail. *She's waiting for a treat,* Idris thought. Philby barked. *Oh no,* Idris thought. *Please stop barking, I don't know what she will do to you if you annoy her.* Philby barked again, lifting her nose in the air. Idris recognized that action, it was what Philby did when she wanted him to look at something. He followed Philby's gaze up into the rafters. What could she have seen that would cause her to act like that?

Idris let his eyes wander over the warehouse. He squinted toward the shelves where he knew Mom was hiding but couldn't see any sign of her. He looked up at the roof space, seeking out any shapes or signs of movement. It was the same technique he used when searching for bird nests in the trees by his house.

Then, suddenly, Idris saw them. With a gasp, he realized exactly what Philby was looking at. A couple of feet in front of the Countess, arms and legs splayed around the beams as if they were hugging them, two scaly bodies were slowly and quietly clambering their way toward the ceiling.

The pangolins had escaped!

Chapter Fourteen

Idris jabbed Lucía in the ribs and pointed urgently toward the pangolins. It took Lucía a moment to spot them but when she did, she let out a gasp.

"What are they doing out of the bag?" she whispered.

"No idea," said Idris. "But we have to make sure the Countess doesn't see them."

Lucía nodded.

"If we don't do something she will see them when she gets into the car."

Idris chewed his bottom lip.

"I'm going in there," Lucía said.

Idris tried to tell her to wait but it was too late—she had jumped up and run into the warehouse before her name had even left his lips.

"Is that a McLaren 570GT?" Lucía squealed, rapidly approaching the Countess and rushing to place her hands on the hood of the car. Idris hoped they hadn't messed everything up by letting the Countess see Lucía.

"**DON'T TOUCH MY CAR!**" The Countess whirled toward Lucía, drawstring sack flailing wildly to one side.

"I'm sorry," said Lucía. "It's just so beautiful." She moved around to the window farthest away from the pangolins. "Is it true that it has a top speed of two hundred miles per hour?"

The Countess scowled, edging around the car and leaning to open what looked like a window on the rear, without taking her eyes off Lucía. The window opened upward to reveal a small trunk space. The countess slung the bag of melons inside. It landed with a thump.

"And can it really go from zero to sixty in just 3.4 seconds?"

"Step away from my car," the Countess replied. Lucía was blocking the driver's door.

"Oh, sorry," babbled Lucía, moving out of the way, stepping carefully between the car and the pangolins so she would block the Countess's view. "Just such a beautiful car. I've never seen a real one before."

"And you never will again," said the Countess. "It's custom made. One of a kind.

Extremely expensive."

The car's doors opened upward, like a ladybug raising its elytra in preparation for flight. Inside, the car's seats were covered in fur. Idris hoped it wasn't real. The Countess folded herself into the driver's seat, then pulled down the mirror to admire her reflection. After rearranging her hair, she started the engine. A rumble like thunder burst from the car's exhaust. Idris let his eyes wander across to the pangolins. They had stopped climbing now and were clinging to a beam just above the front of the Countess's car. *Please don't look,* he willed her. *Please don't notice them.*

His eyes flicked back to the car again. The Countess was preparing to drive away. The simplest way to leave the warehouse

would be to drive straight ahead, passing beneath the pangolins, but Lucía was blocking her way.

"**MOVE, GIRL!**" screeched the Countess, barely audible over the sound of her car's engine.

"What's that?" said Lucía. She pointed to her hearing aid. "I can't hear you."

The Countess shook her fist in the air and fiddled with the car's controls. The car made an even louder roar, then shot backward. Philby raced after it, barking loudly.

"**Come back, Philby!**'" shouted Lucía. But the car had already zoomed off into the distance.

Idris let out a long breath. The Countess had fallen for it! He felt a grin break out across his face. Now she could drive the melons to wherever she wanted. The pangolins were safe!

Mom emerged from behind the shelves, holding her smartphone in her hand.

"Front row seats for the best show in town!" she declared. "Very quick thinking, Lucía. I thought for a moment the Countess was going to spot the pangolins, but you managed to keep her totally focused on your little act."

Lucía gave a little bow.

"And whose idea was it to give the sack to Philby?"

Lucía pointed at Idris.

"That's my boy," Mom said, pulling Idris toward her in a hug. "What a team we make, eh?"

"Not bad for a couple of kids, huh?" said Lucía. She nudged Idris on the arm, "I told you that you could be good at this."

"Not bad at all," said Mom.

"So Lucía's not in trouble for letting the Countess see her?" Idris asked.

"Not at all," said Mom. "That was very smart thinking. In fact," she raised her eyebrows up and down as if she was about to say something exciting. "I'm so impressed, I was wondering if you would consider officially joining my team."

"What?!" said Idris and Lucía together.

"Well, you know what I do now, and you've proved you both have valuable skills."

"You mean," said Lucía, "be *actual* spies?"

"That's right," said Mom.

Lucía gave a high pitched scream.

"I don't know whether to faint or laugh or cry," she said.

"I'll take that as a yes," said Mom. "And what about you, Idris? I could use someone with your observation skills."

Idris thought about the adventure they had just shared. Sure, at moments it had been dangerous and he'd never felt so frightened in his life before, but at other times it had actually been pretty fun...

"Only if you can promise me you'll never ever get kidnapped again," said Idris. "I was so worried. I'm not sure I can go through that again."

"I'll do my best," said Mom. "That much I can promise."

"So what now," said Lucía, "do we have an initiation or—"

"Well, there is the small matter of figuring out what your agent names will be. As you know, I'm agent Maned Wolf and my associate is Agent Walrus. Perhaps you could both think about which animals you would like to be."

Lucía looked ready to answer immediately but Idris raised his hand.

"A decision as big as this one requires some serious thought. Can I think about it and get back to you?"

"Of course you can," said Mom. "In the meantime, shall we get these sassy little creatures down?" She pointed up at the pangolins.

Idris smiled.

"I'll get them," he said.

"How did they escape?" Lucía asked.

"I think they were fed up of being inside the bag," Mom said, holding up the ripped shreds of a drawstring sack.

"They must be really hungry," said Idris, passing the first pangolin to Lucía. "Let's get them back to their enclosure. Maybe Victor can show us what to feed them."

He carefully retrieved the second pangolin. As he passed it to Mom, its long tongue emerged from its mouth and touched him gently on the arm.

"What is that?!" Lucía squealed.

"Its tongue," said Idris.

"But it's so long," said Lucía.

"Longer than its whole body," said Idris. "Perfect for scooping up ants." He stroked the pangolin's scales, noting the hair that stuck out between them. "We'll get you some food soon," he said. "Don't worry."

"I can't believe anyone would hurt these little things," said Lucía. "I'm so glad they are safe now."

"It's all thanks to you two," said Mom. "You saved them."

"And Philby," Lucía reminded her.

"And Philby," Mom laughed. "I couldn't be prouder of the three of you." She pulled all of them, including Philby, in for a tight hug. It might have gone on for longer, but they were interrupted by somebody's rumbling stomach.

"This spying is hungry work," said Lucía. "Anyone want a quesadilla?"

Chapter Fifteen

Three weeks later, after recovering in the veterinary center, the pangolins had been cleared for release back into their enclosure. In the time they had been away, Victor had taken the opportunity to renovate their space and installed two new trees and a cozy treehouse for them to relax in. It looked fantastic. Idris, Lucía, Mom, and Dad had all been invited to the grand re-opening.

"What do you think?" Victor asked, striding toward them wearing a yellow T-shirt that said *Save the Pangolins* and a smile from ear to ear.

"It looks fantastic, Victor," said Lucía.

"The pangolins are going to love it," Idris agreed.

After a short speech about how grateful the zoo was for Victor's continued service and their relief at having the pangolins returned safe and sound, the pangolins were released back into their home. They immediately started sniffing around the base of the new trees and within minutes, one of them had begun to climb.

"Look how happy they look," said Lucía.

"All thanks to you two," Mom whispered.

"What are you three whispering about?" said David, still in his veterinary scrubs.

"Hi, David," said Idris. "How was work?"

"Not bad at all," said David. "You know, it's strange, but ever since the pangolins have been found safely, Budi has gone completely back to normal. It's almost like he missed them or something."

Lucía and Idris shared a look.

"Or something..." mouthed Lucía.

Idris stifled a giggle.

"I'm not surprised he was miserable with that awful woman clambering in and out of his cage on a daily basis," whispered Idris. "I think I'd lose my appetite in that situation too."

"I know," replied Lucía. "She chills me to the core. Although..." She let out a sigh. "You have to admit her car was pretty cool."

Idris shrugged and shook his head. "I didn't think it was that great. Zero to sixty in 3.4 seconds—is that what you said?"

"Yep," said Lucía. "Can you imagine?"

"If you find that impressive?" Idris said.

"Then wait till I tell you about the acceleration on a cheetah!"

Lucía flashed him an excited smile.

"OK," she said eagerly. "Maybe we can talk about it this weekend?"

Idris nodded. He knew exactly which episode of *Creature Feature* he was going to show her to demonstrate the wonders of the world's fastest land animal.

"Can't wait," he said with a smile. "And I've got a new trick to teach Philby too."

"Amazing," said Lucía. "Sounds like the best weekend ever."

Mom appeared over Lucía's shoulder.

"I have some news," she said, pulling the children away from the crowd. "Someone filed a report about a drawstring sack full of melons and pineapples dumped outside an airport."

"An airport," said Lucía, "do we think 'you know who' has traveled somewhere abroad?"

"We're investigating several leads at the moment but the truth is we just don't know what she is planning," said Mom. Her voice was barely louder than a whisper. "There's lots more work to do."

"We're ready to help, if you need us," said Idris.

Mom smiled.

"I was hoping you would say that. Have you given any thought to that thing I asked you about? You know, *the names*..."

Idris and Lucía shared a look. They had spent a whole afternoon poring over Idris's animal encyclopedia, weighing up the talents and skills of various different species. They had both made shortlists of several different animals, but in the end only one name had felt right for each of them.

"We have," said Lucía.

The two children gave each other a nod, then each of them struck a pose before saying…

"Agent Hawk and Agent Wolf Cub reporting for duty."

The adventure continues in:

ANDY MCNAB

JESS FRENCH

ILLUSTRATED BY NATHAN REED